Sir Whong and the Golden Pig

adapted by *Oki S. Han*
and *Stephanie Haboush Plunkett*

PICTURES BY Oki S. Han

Dial Books for Young Readers New York

To J.C., who is the light of my life;
Mom and Dad; my husband Sun and baby Joseph
O.S.H.

For Mom and Dad, and for Richard
S.H.P.

———————————————

Published by Dial Books for Young Readers
A Division of Penguin Books USA Inc.
375 Hudson Street | New York, New York 10014

Copyright © 1993 by Oki S. Han
All rights reserved | Typography by Amelia Lau Carling
Printed in Hong Kong
by South China Printing Company (1988) Limited
First Edition
1 3 5 7 9 10 8 6 4 2

Library of Congress Cataloging in Publication Data
Han, Oki S.
Sir Whong and the golden pig |
adapted by Oki S. Han and Stephanie Haboush Plunkett ;
pictures by Oki S. Han.—1st ed.
p. cm.
Adapted from an ancient Korean tale.
Summary: When he manages to get a loan of one
thousand nyung by giving a fake golden pig as collateral,
a stranger thinks that he has outwitted
the wise and generous Sir Whong.
ISBN 0-8037-1344-4 (tr.)—ISBN 0-8037-1345-2 (lib.)
[1. Folklore—Korea. 2. Swindlers and swindling—Folklore.]
I. Plunkett, Stephanie Haboush. II. Title.
PZ8.1.H158Si 1993 398.2—dc20 [E] 91-43389 CIP AC

The art for each picture consists of a watercolor painting,
which is scanner-separated and reproduced in full color.

⚍ Some Facts About Ancient Korea ⚍

Money · Ancient Korean money, called nyung, was made of copper and had a hole in its center so that it could easily be carried strung on a cord.

The Alphabet · In ancient Korea, Chinese characters were used in writing. A Korean written alphabet was not established until 1446.

The Wedding Ceremony · Marriages were arranged by the bride's and groom's families, and the couple did not meet until their wedding day. (For example, Oki Han's maternal grandparents' marriage was arranged by their families, who decided at the births of their children that they would wed.) The bride and groom were dressed in elaborate ceremonial clothing and were physically supported by members of their families as they bowed deeply to each other for the first time. Beautifully painted screens added color to the gathering and special ceremonial objects were arranged near the couple. The rooster and the hen represented mythological birds that in Korean lore were lifetime mates. A red cloth symbolic of the bride was wrapped around the rooster and a blue cloth representing the groom was wrapped around the hen to show that the two were joined. The everlasting union was reiterated in male and female ducks, which were identified by their red and blue coloring, and also by the white vase holding evergreen and bamboo branches. A wild goose brought to the ceremony by the groom meant that he would always provide for his wife and their children.

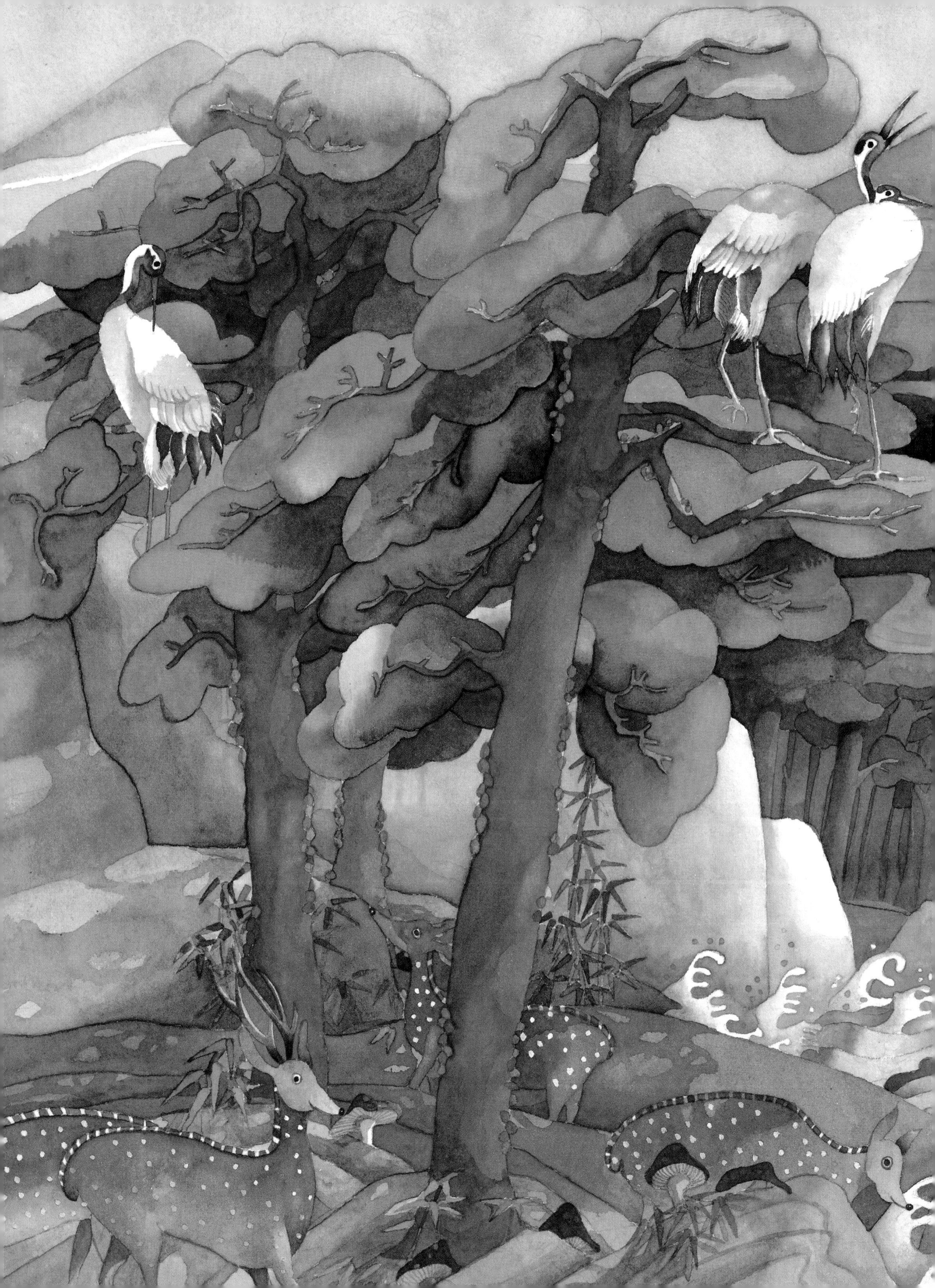

A long, long time ago in Korea, the ancient country of quiet beauty, there lived a man named Sir Whong.

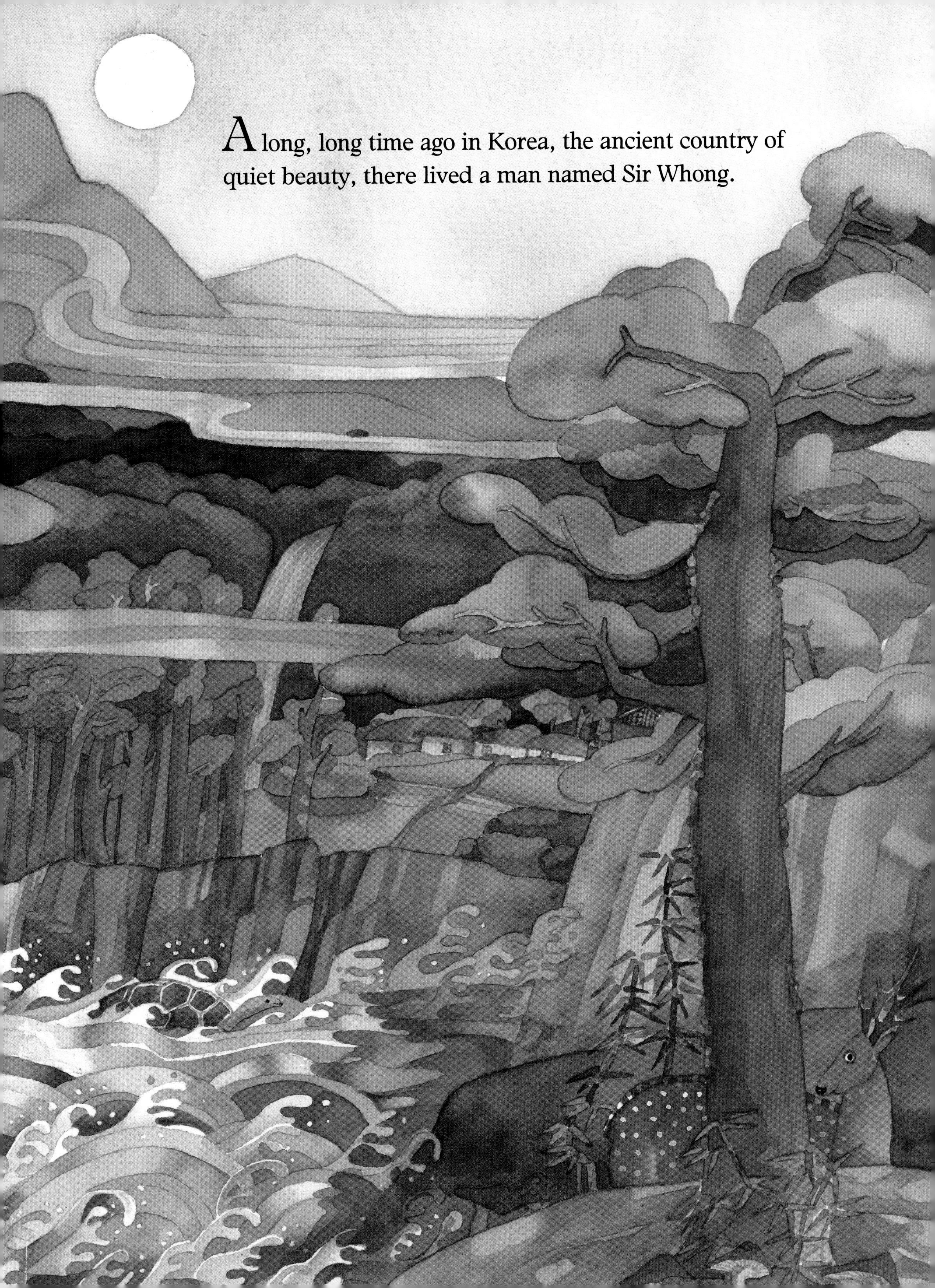

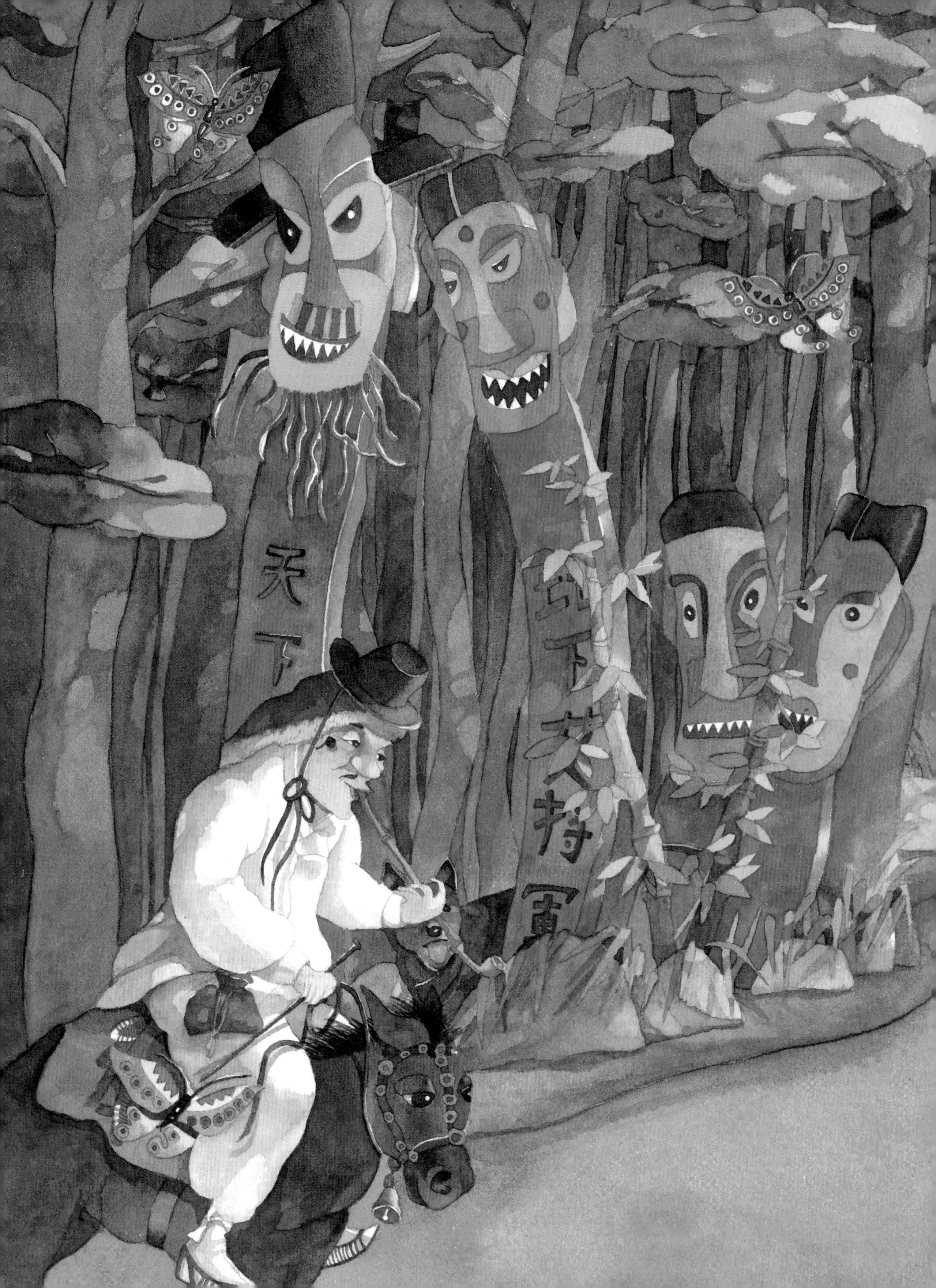
天下
地下女将軍

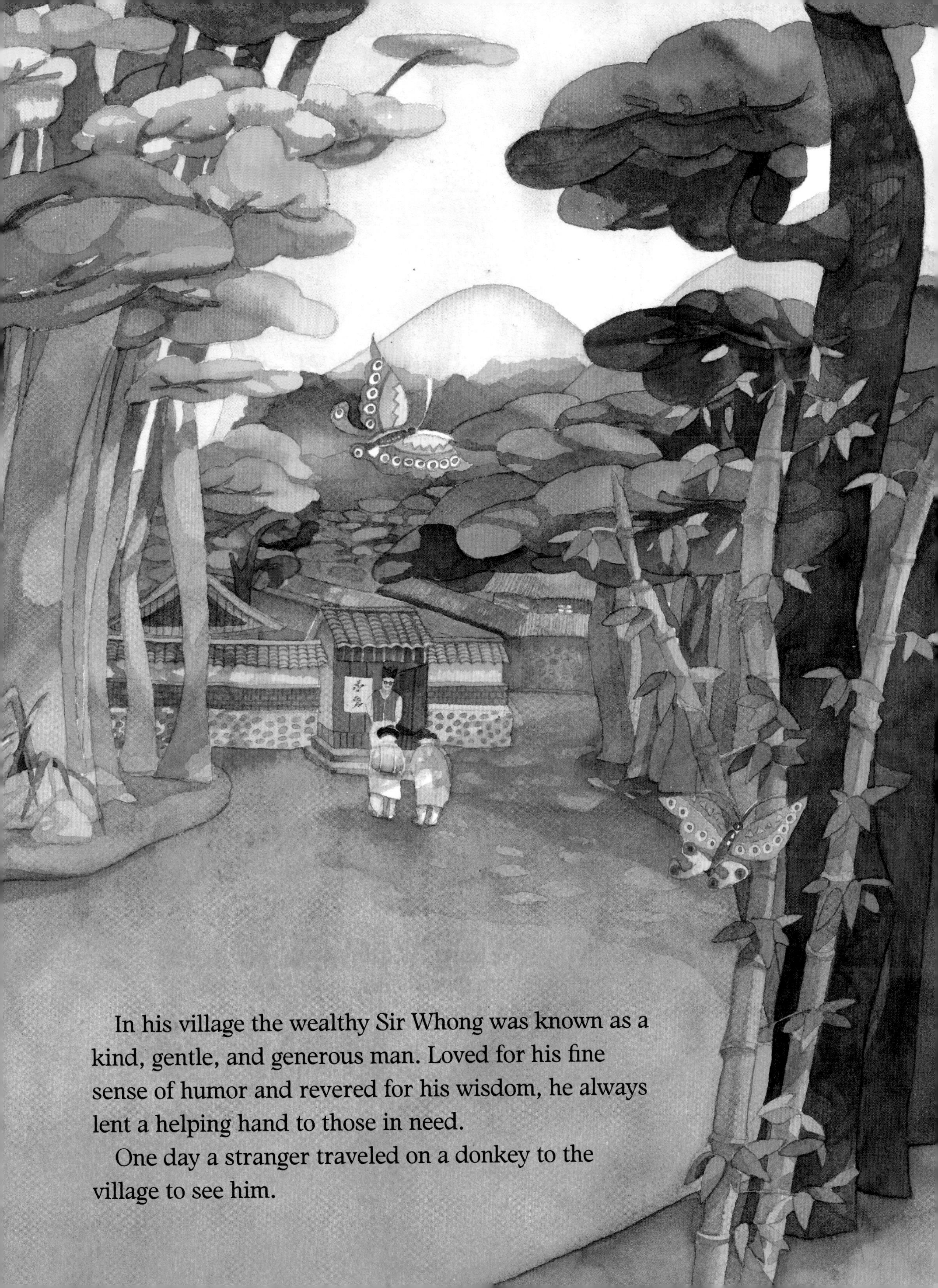

In his village the wealthy Sir Whong was known as a kind, gentle, and generous man. Loved for his fine sense of humor and revered for his wisdom, he always lent a helping hand to those in need.

One day a stranger traveled on a donkey to the village to see him.

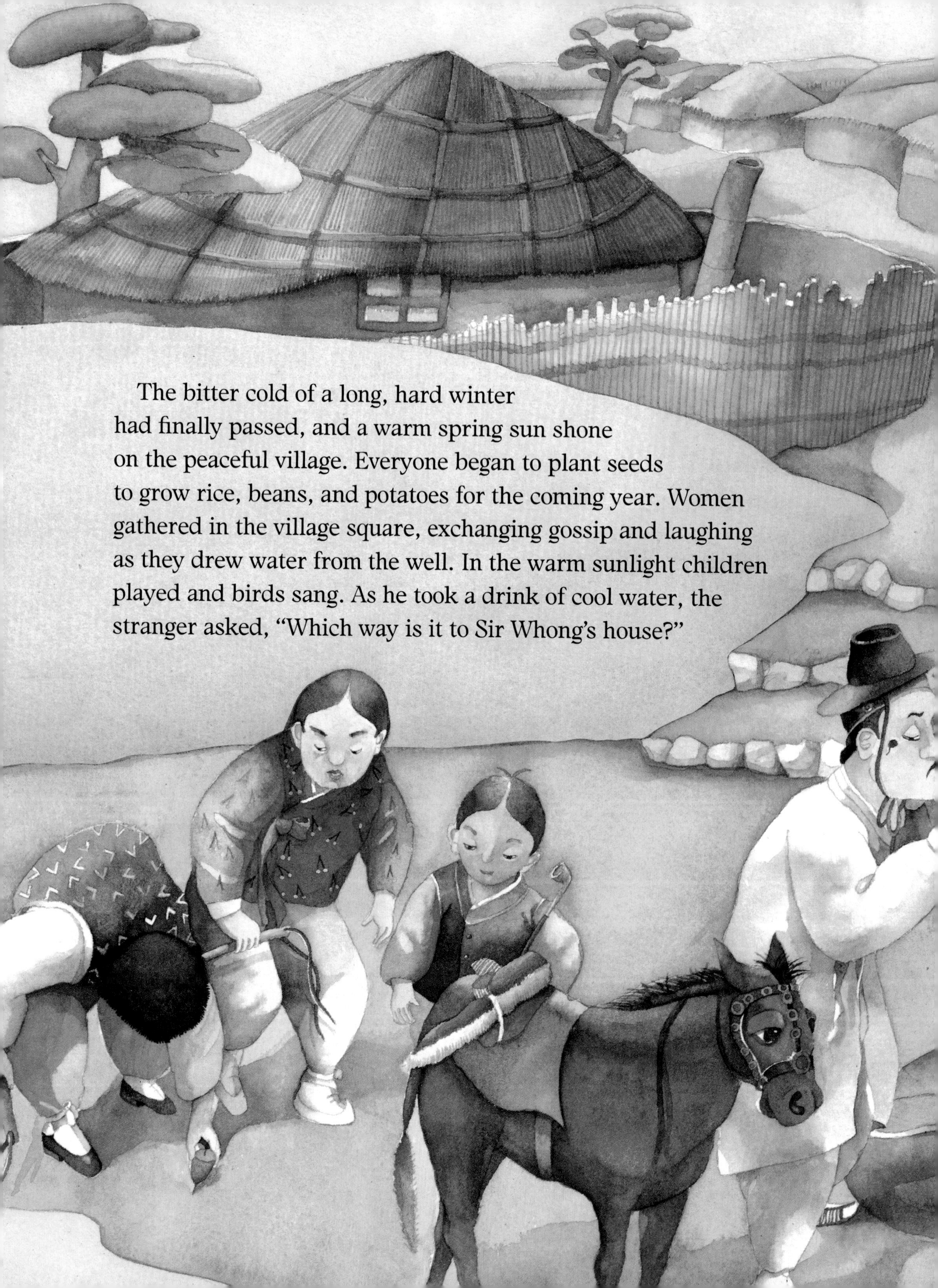

The bitter cold of a long, hard winter had finally passed, and a warm spring sun shone on the peaceful village. Everyone began to plant seeds to grow rice, beans, and potatoes for the coming year. Women gathered in the village square, exchanging gossip and laughing as they drew water from the well. In the warm sunlight children played and birds sang. As he took a drink of cool water, the stranger asked, “Which way is it to Sir Whong’s house?”

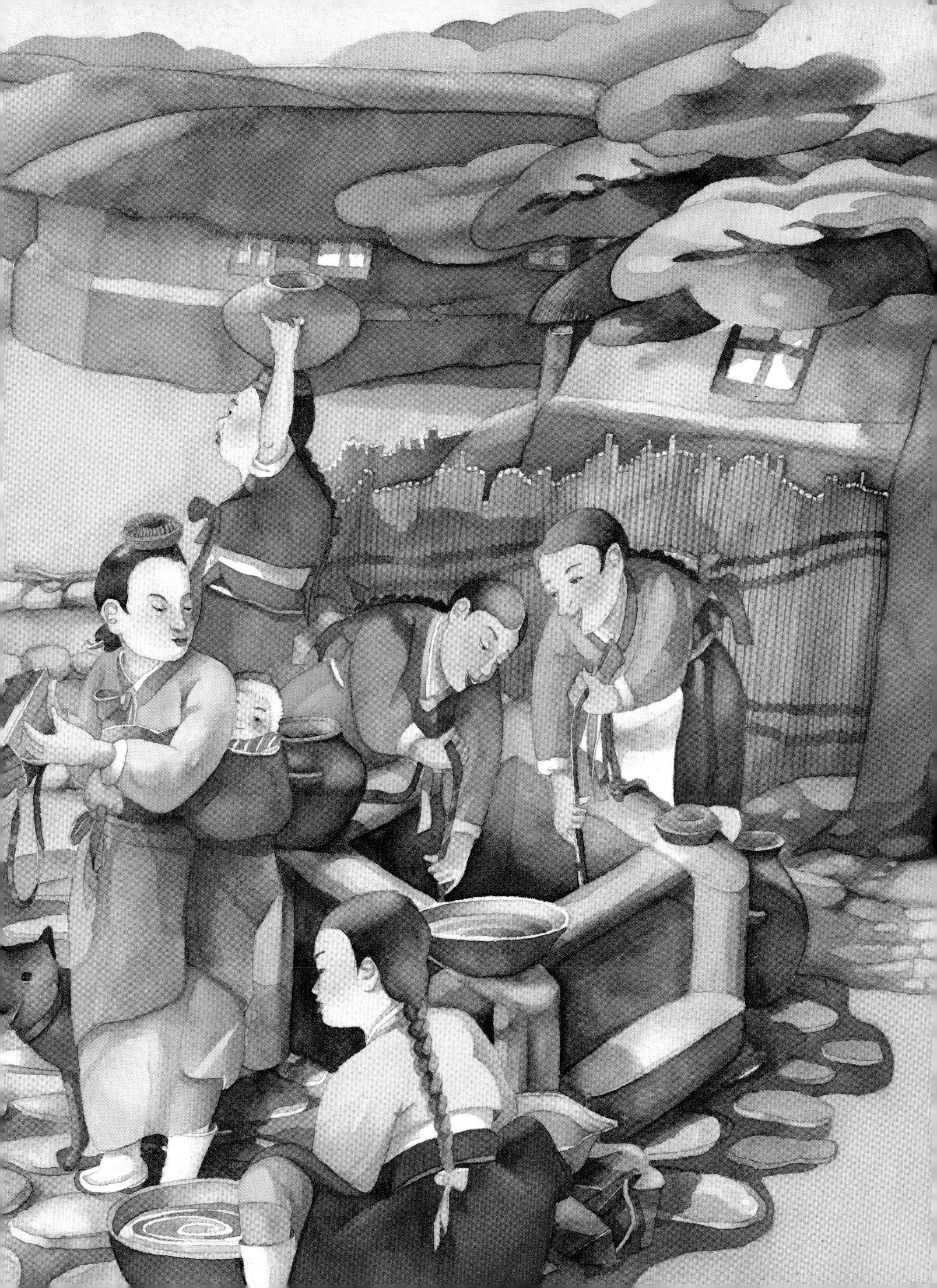

After a while the stranger arrived at Sir Whong's gate. He must have been from far away, for no one recognized him.

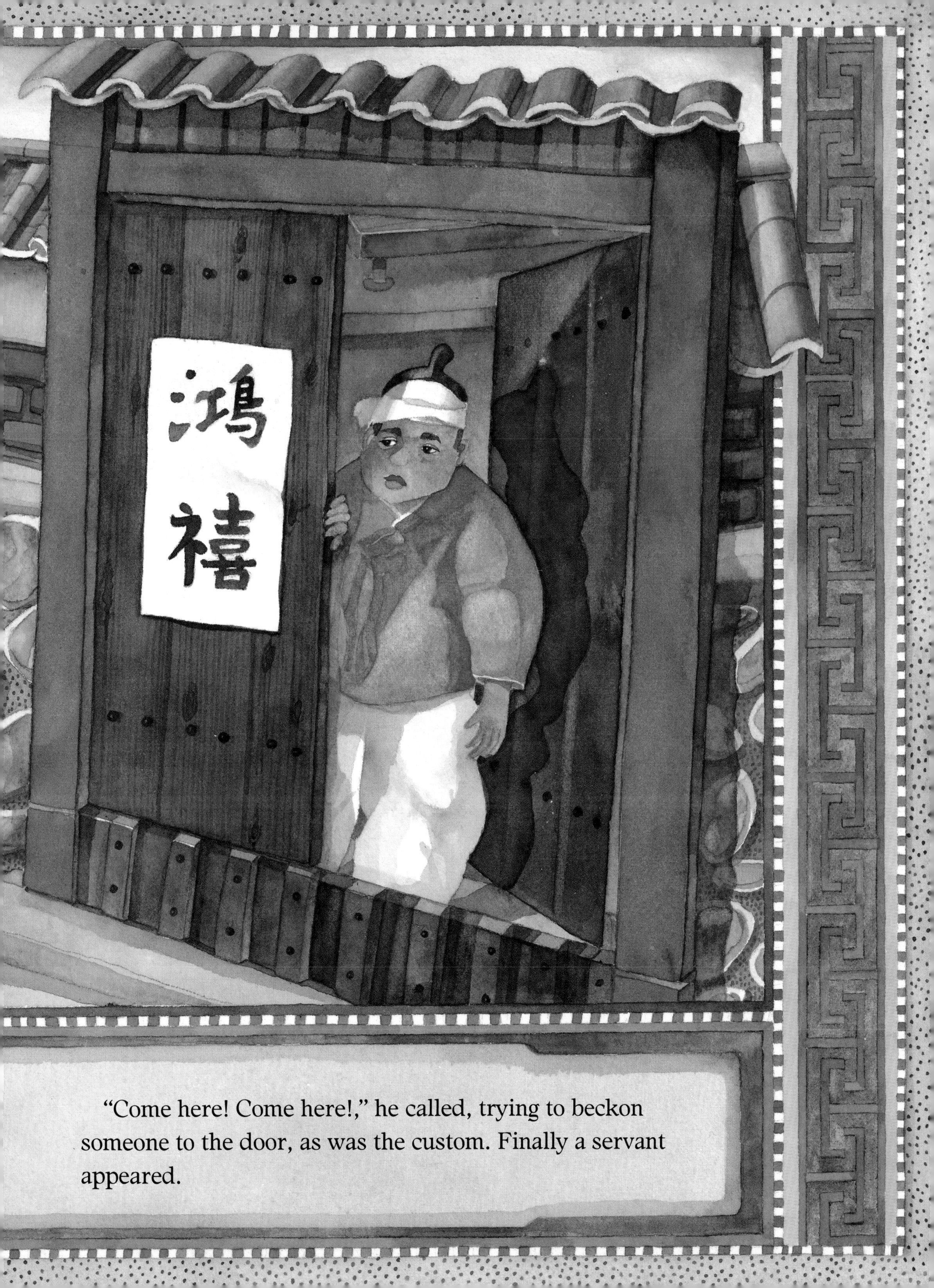
鴻
禧

"Come here! Come here!," he called, trying to beckon someone to the door, as was the custom. Finally a servant appeared.

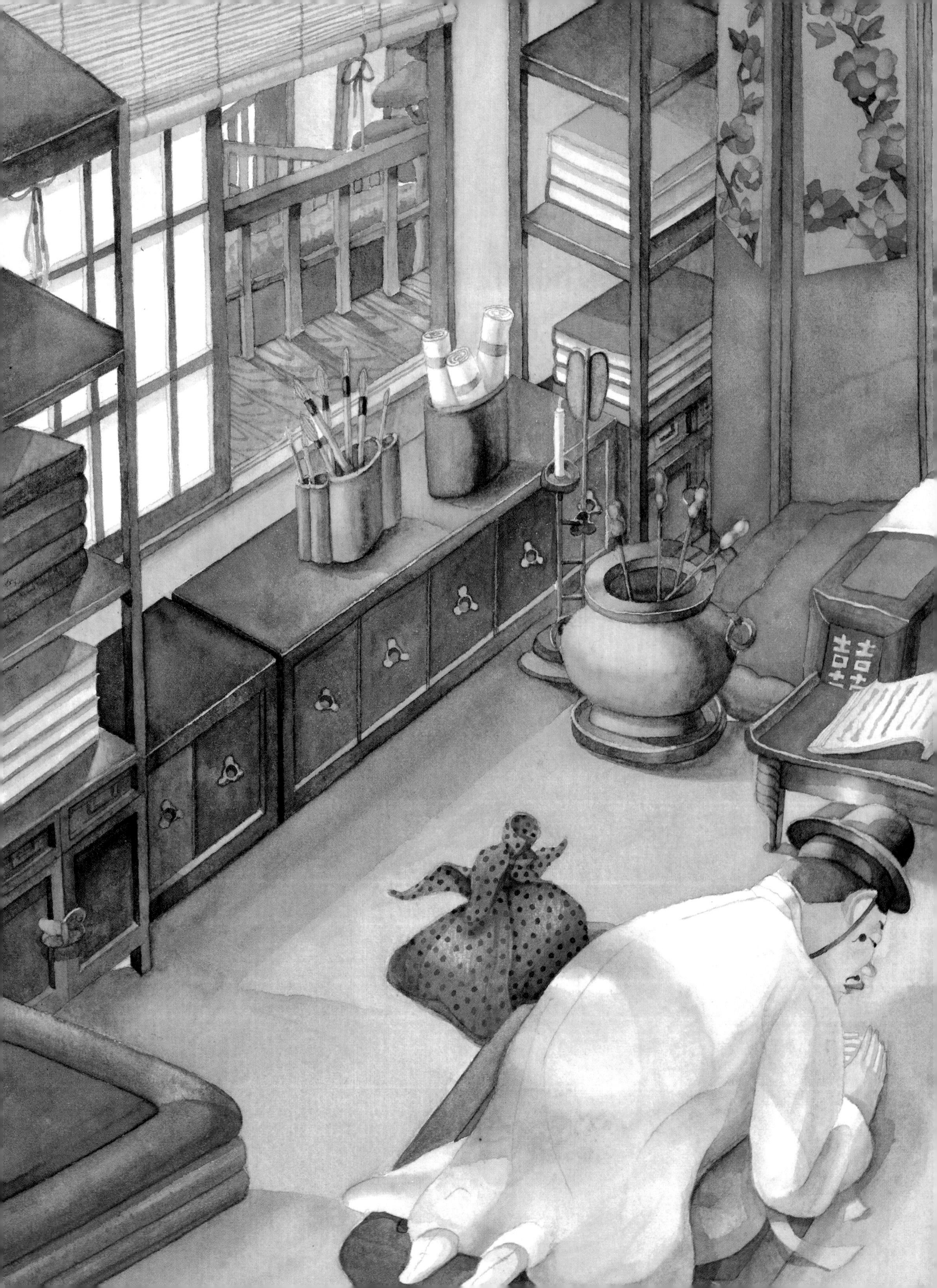

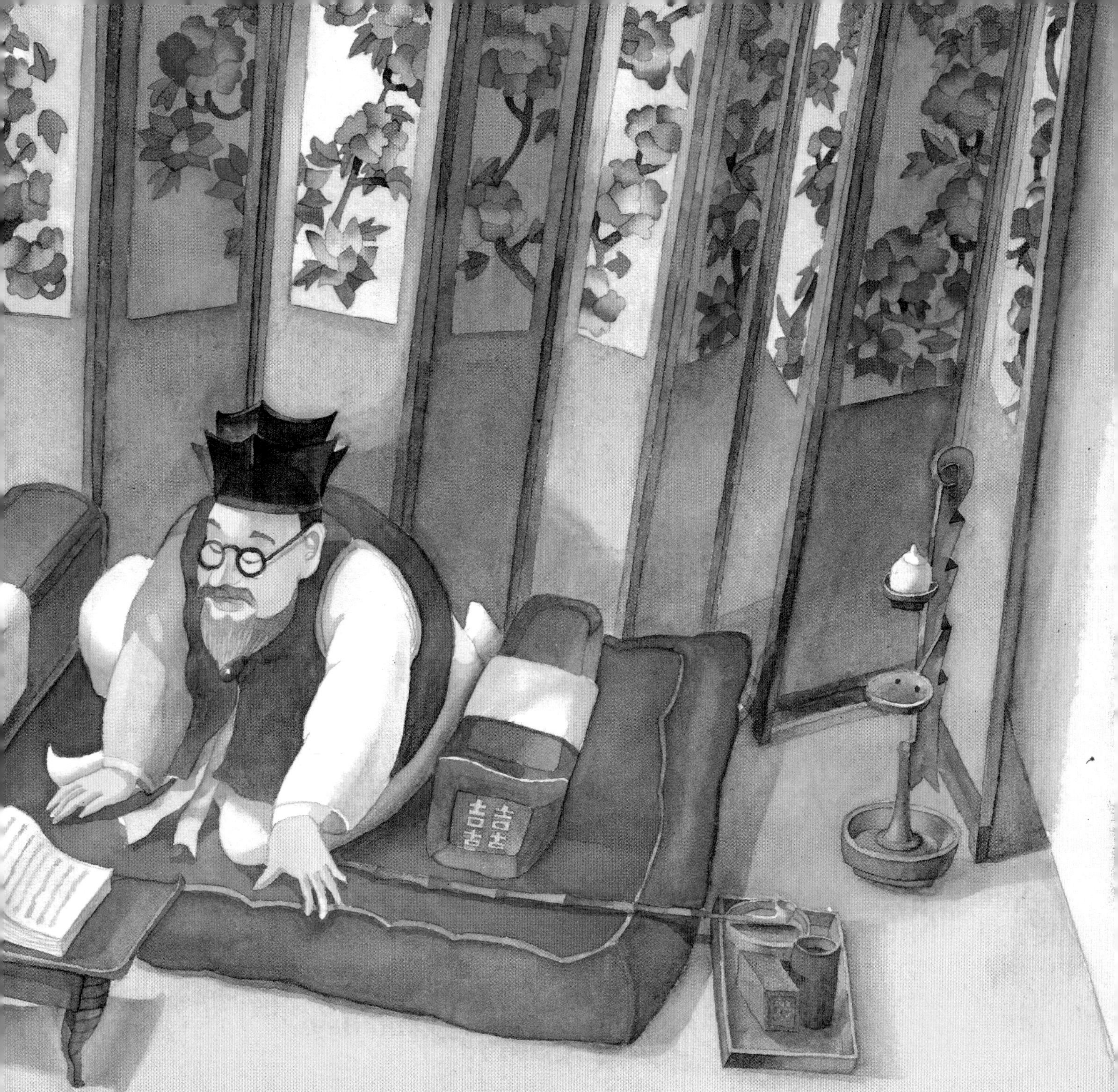

The servant led the stranger into an elegant room where Sir Whong entertained his guests. The room was filled with objects of great beauty that reflected his good taste. Fine brushes and rice-paper scrolls were arranged neatly by the window. Artfully carved wooden candlesticks provided light in the evening, and a brass coal stove gave warmth. When Sir Whong entered the room, he and the stranger bowed to each other in greeting.

"My name is Oh," the stranger said, and boldly stated that he wished to borrow money from Sir Whong — one thousand nyung, a great deal of money. So much, in fact, that it was more than the average person could earn in a whole year! Sir Whong was shocked by the stranger's presumption. "What did you say?! One thousand nyung?!" He wondered how a man he did not even know could make such a request.

Mr. Oh began his story. "I live many miles from here. My poor, old mother has been ill for many years. A few days ago a doctor recommended some new medicine that would surely make her well, but alas, it is extremely expensive. It costs one thousand nyung, and I haven't the money. Your generosity is known far and wide, Sir Whong. That is why I have come to you."

Now Sir Whong was a generous man, but giving one thousand nyung to a stranger was most unusual. Quickly Mr. Oh added, "I know that I have asked for a great deal of money. That is why I brought you something special, to show you that I will pay it back." He revealed a box that was wrapped in an old but beautiful fabric.

With great pride he explained that the box held
a treasure that had been in his family for two thousand
years. It was their most prized possession, and could
never be sold. "Of course, if a price could be put on it,"
he said, "it would be worth much more than one
thousand nyung. I will be back in one year to return
the money. Until then, you may keep this treasure as
security." He unwrapped the box carefully. Inside was
a glimmering golden pig that shone as bright as the sun.

Astonished by its beauty and convinced of Mr. Oh's
sincerity, Sir Whong agreed to give him the money.

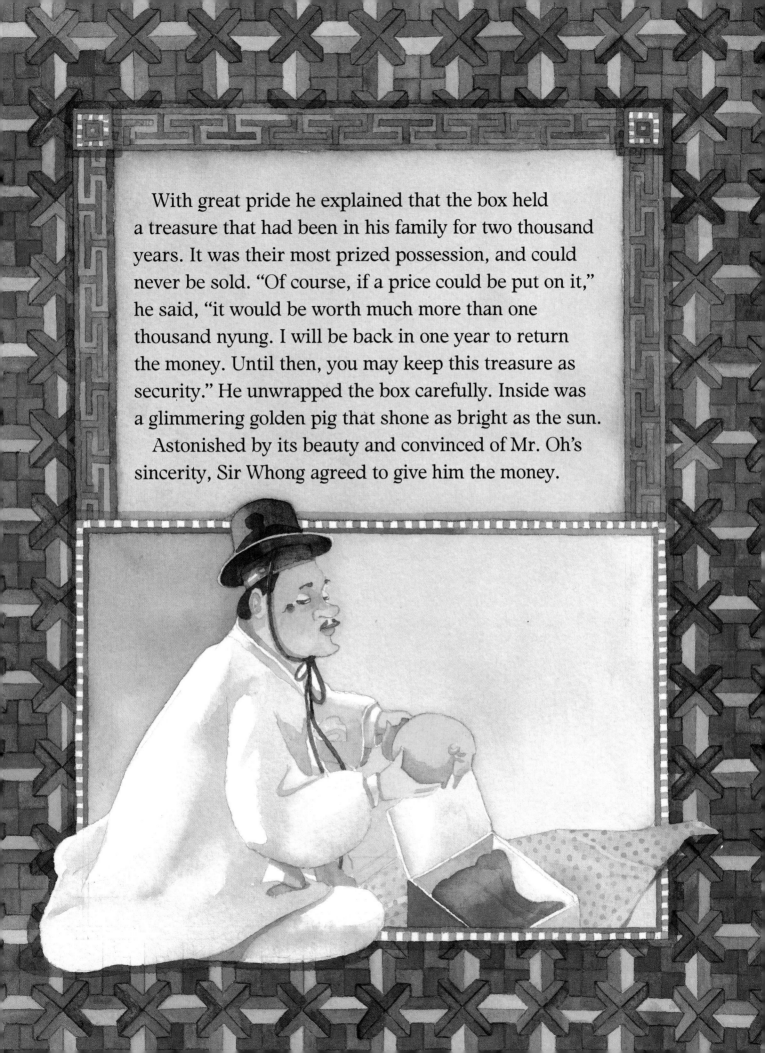

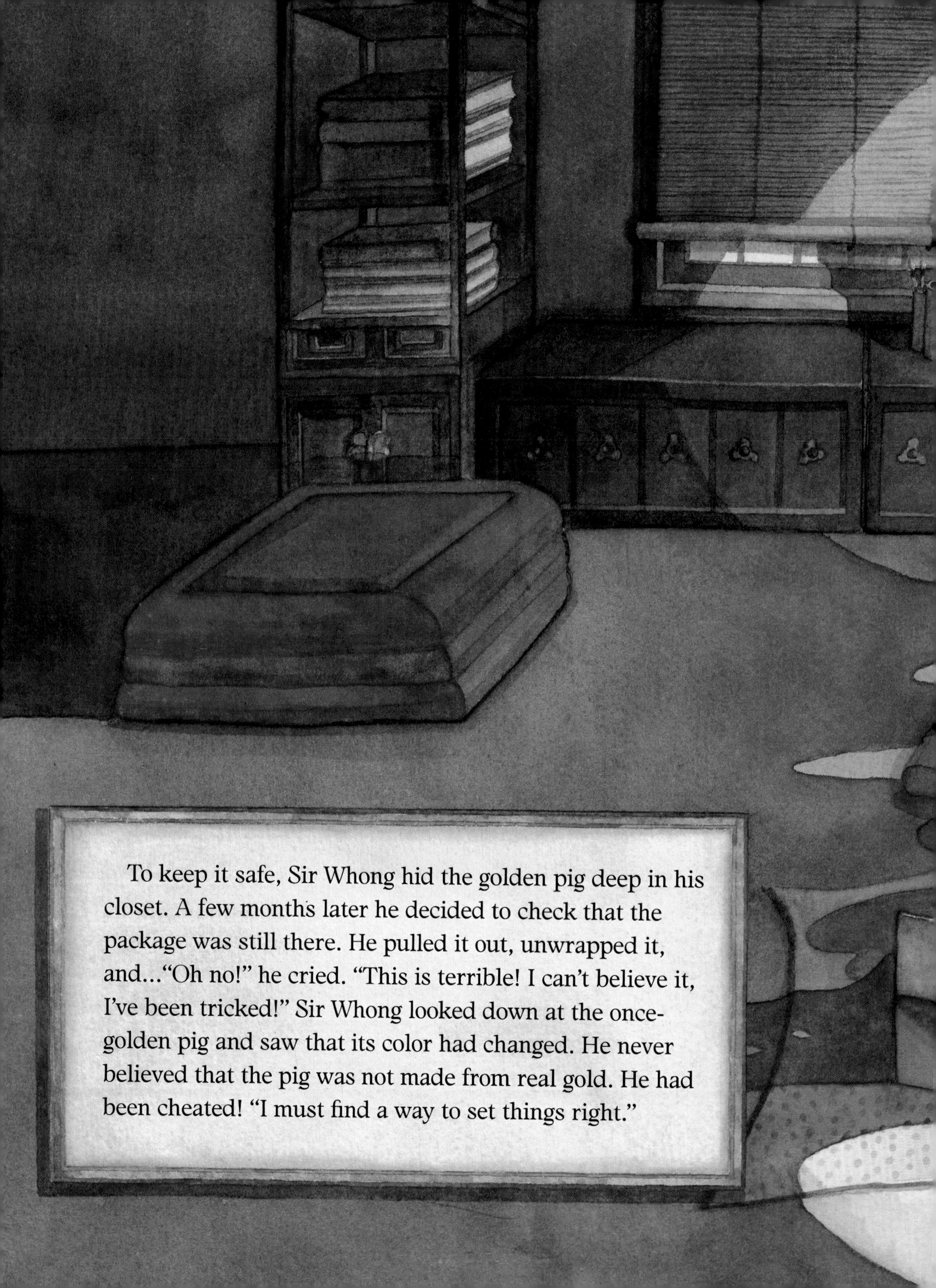

To keep it safe, Sir Whong hid the golden pig deep in his closet. A few months later he decided to check that the package was still there. He pulled it out, unwrapped it, and..."Oh no!" he cried. "This is terrible! I can't believe it, I've been tricked!" Sir Whong looked down at the once-golden pig and saw that its color had changed. He never believed that the pig was not made from real gold. He had been cheated! "I must find a way to set things right."

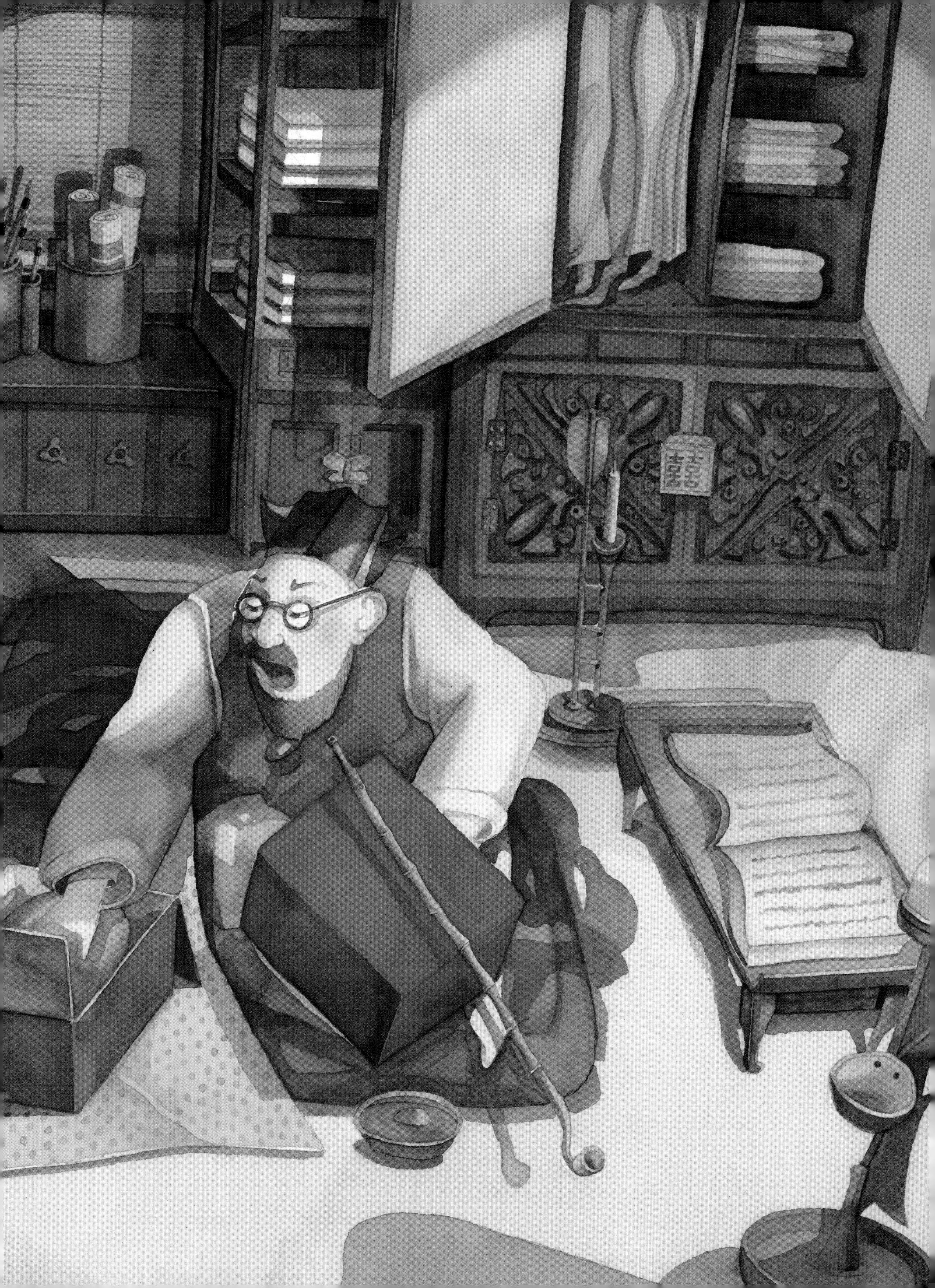
囍

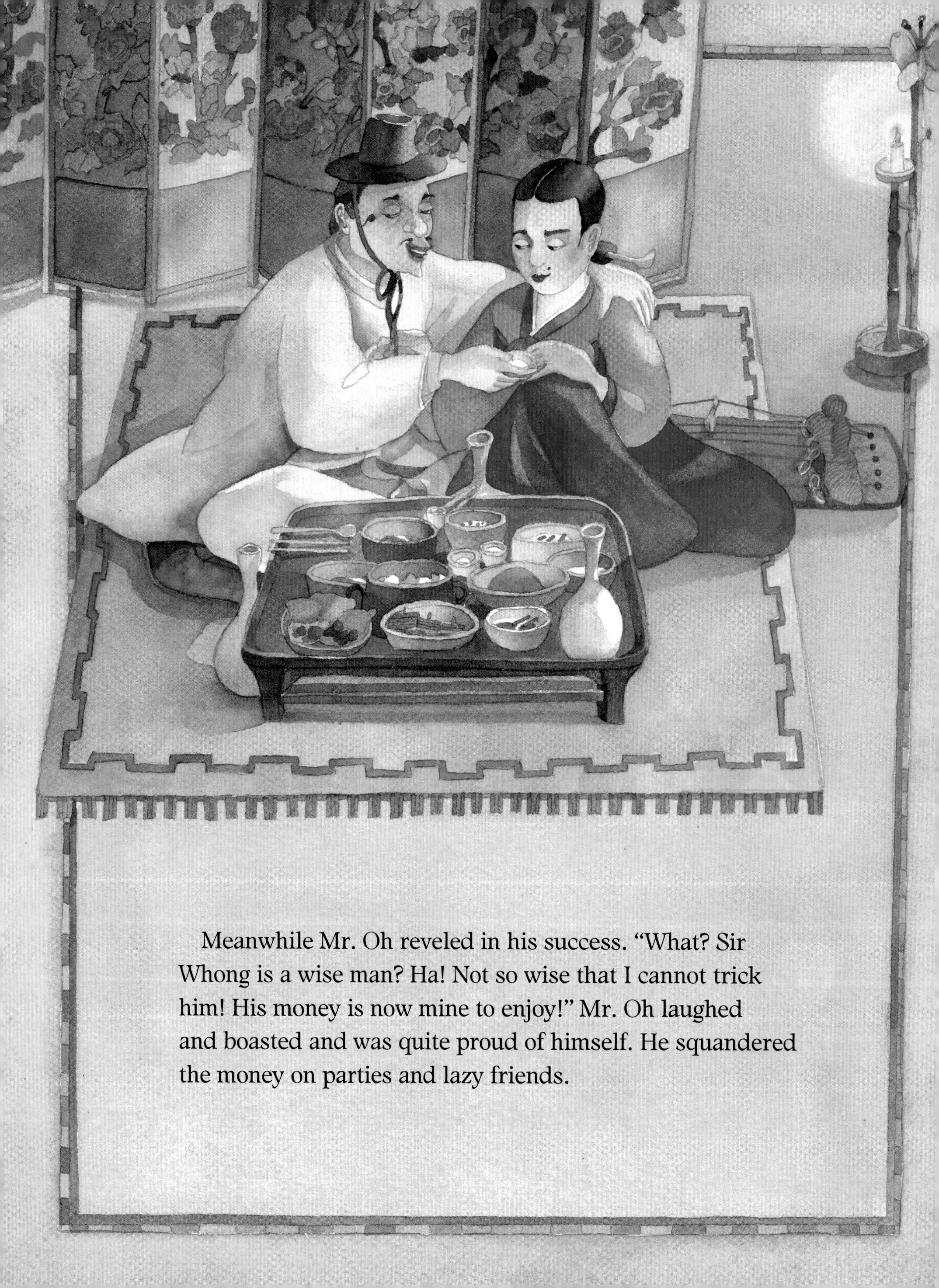

Meanwhile Mr. Oh reveled in his success. “What? Sir Whong is a wise man? Ha! Not so wise that I cannot trick him! His money is now mine to enjoy!” Mr. Oh laughed and boasted and was quite proud of himself. He squandered the money on parties and lazy friends.

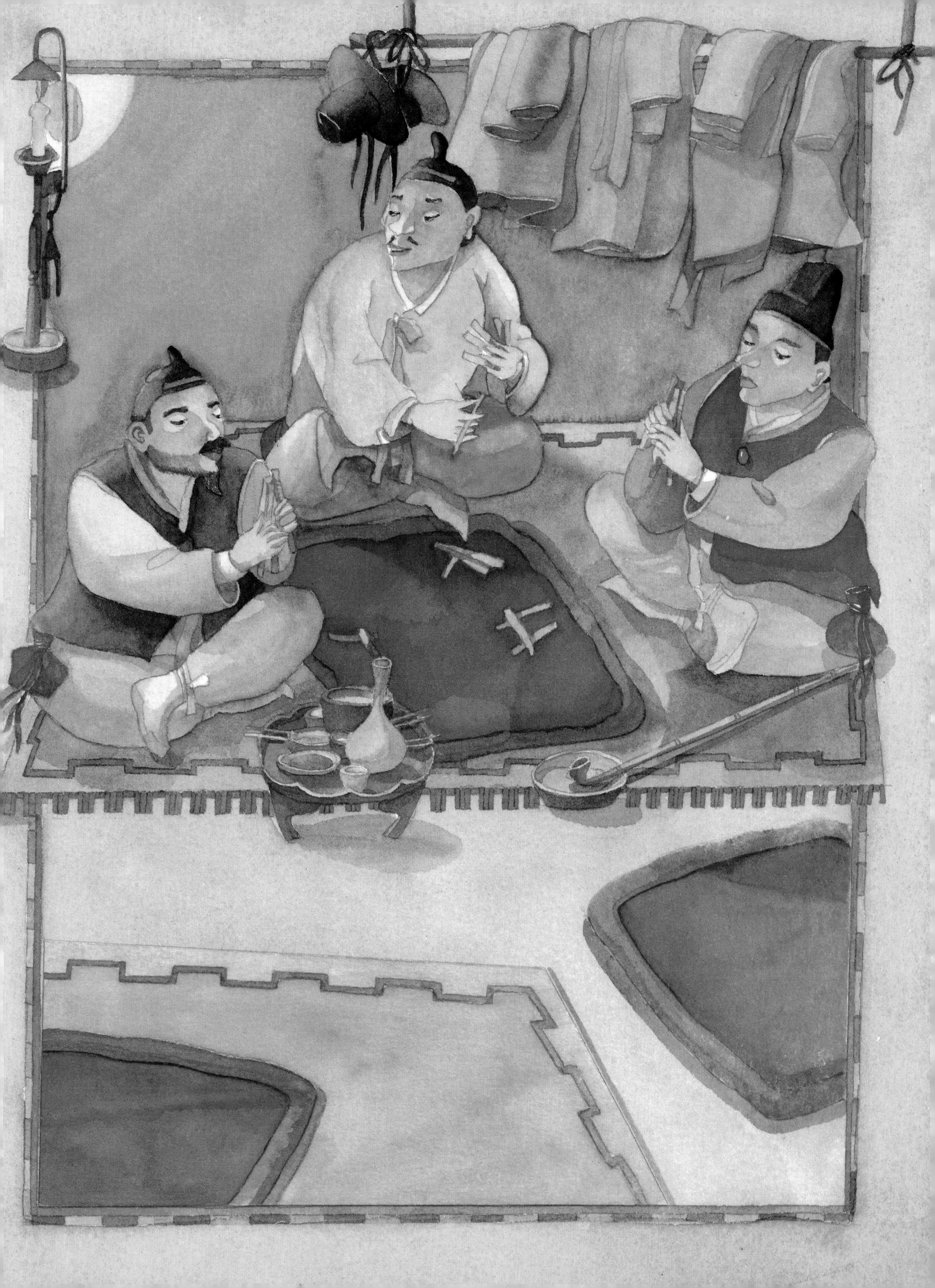

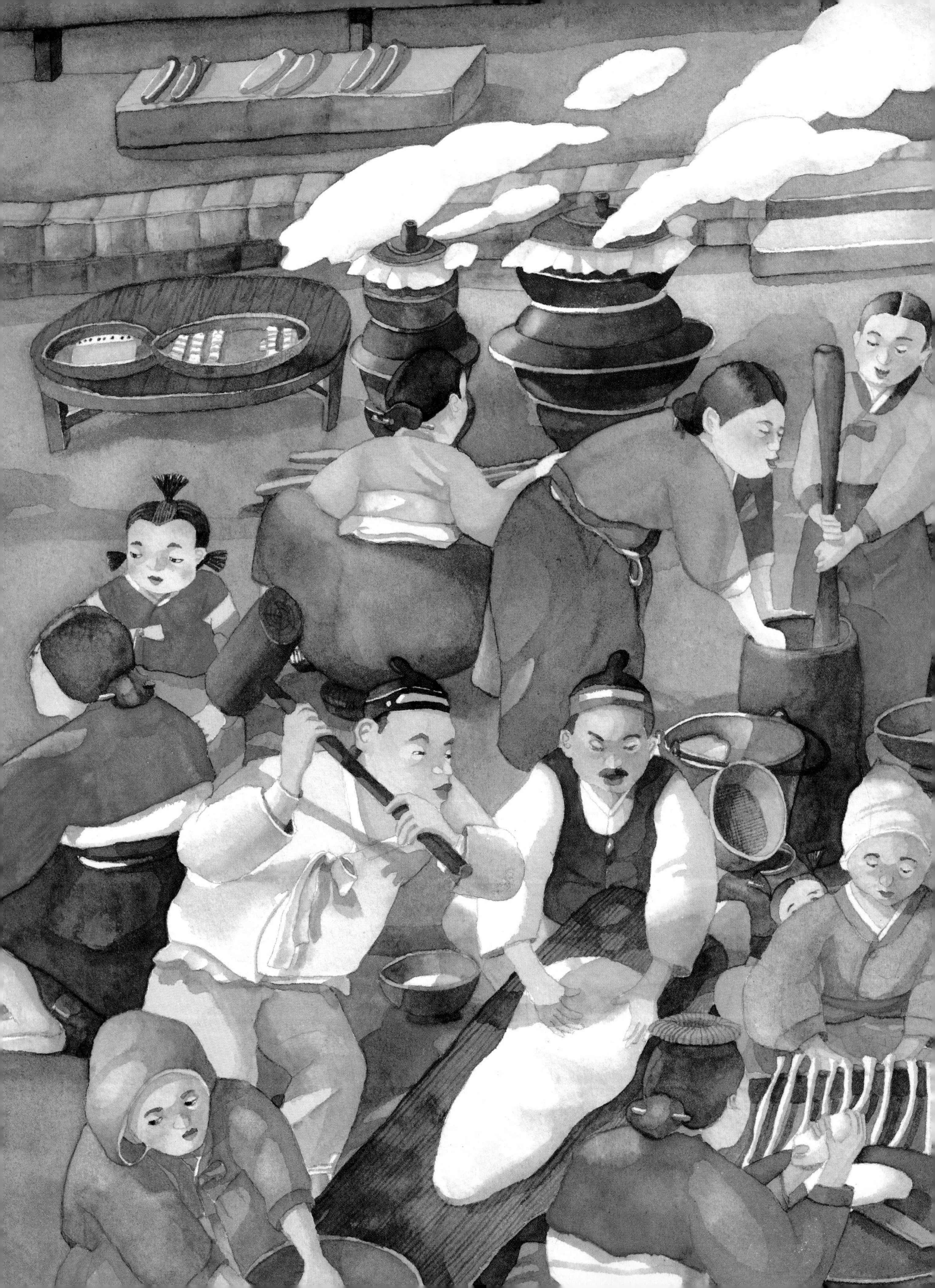

Soon after, a big wedding ceremony was to be held in the village. Everyone gladly worked together for days in preparation of the event. They made special foods for the wedding feast, and built tents to shade the guests or protect them if it rained. In the meantime Sir Whong was devising his *own* plan for the reception.

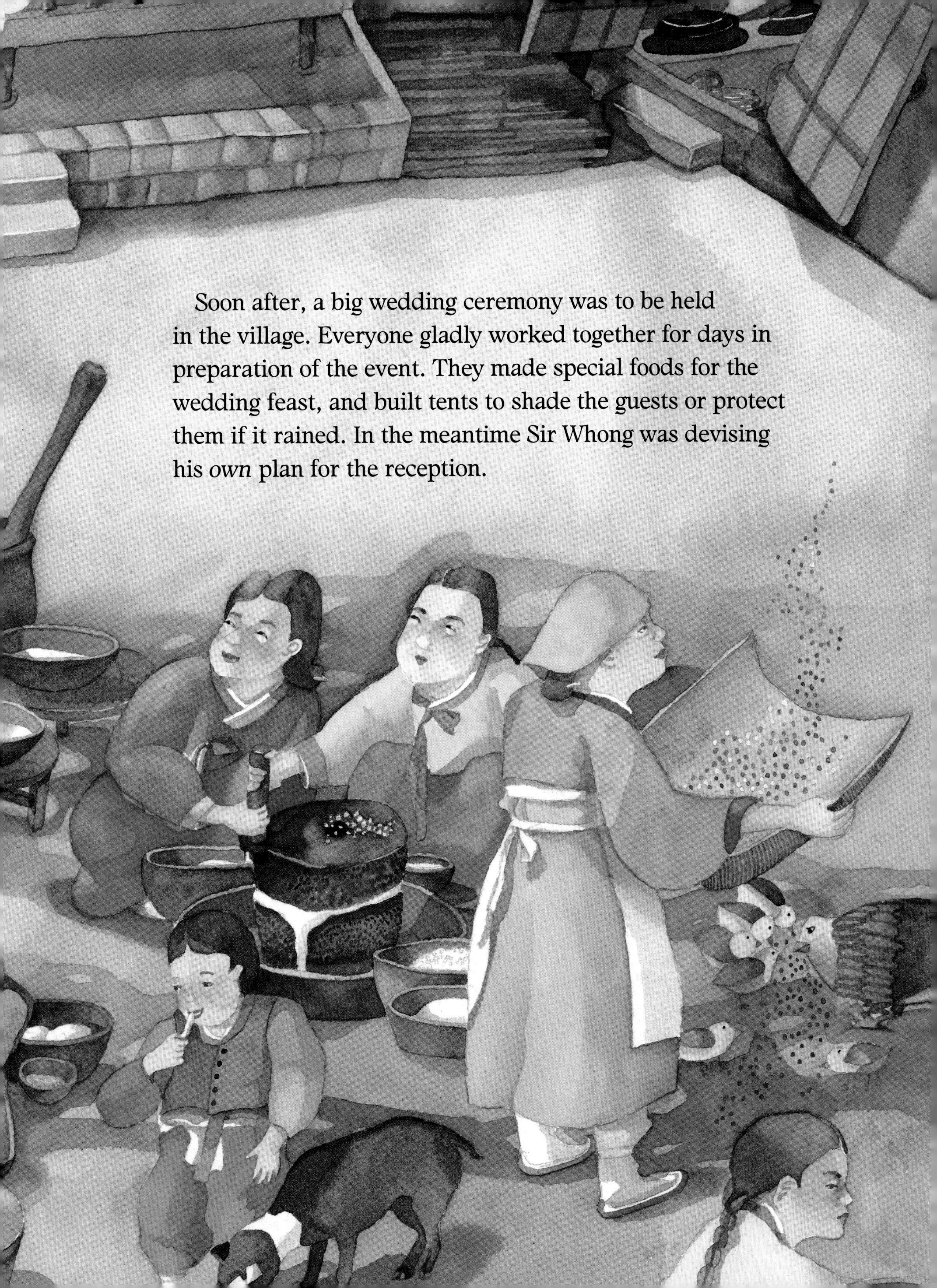

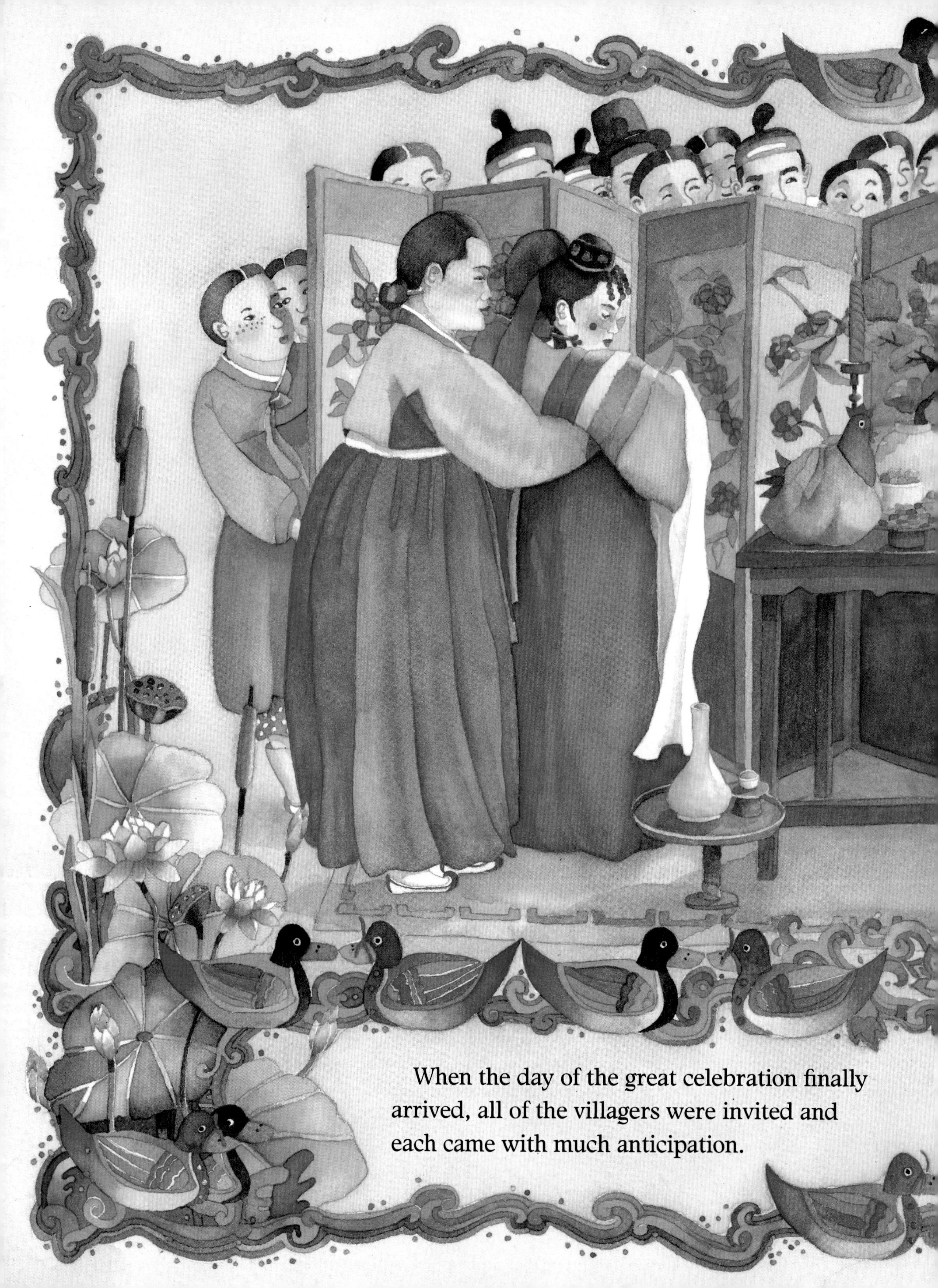

When the day of the great celebration finally arrived, all of the villagers were invited and each came with much anticipation.

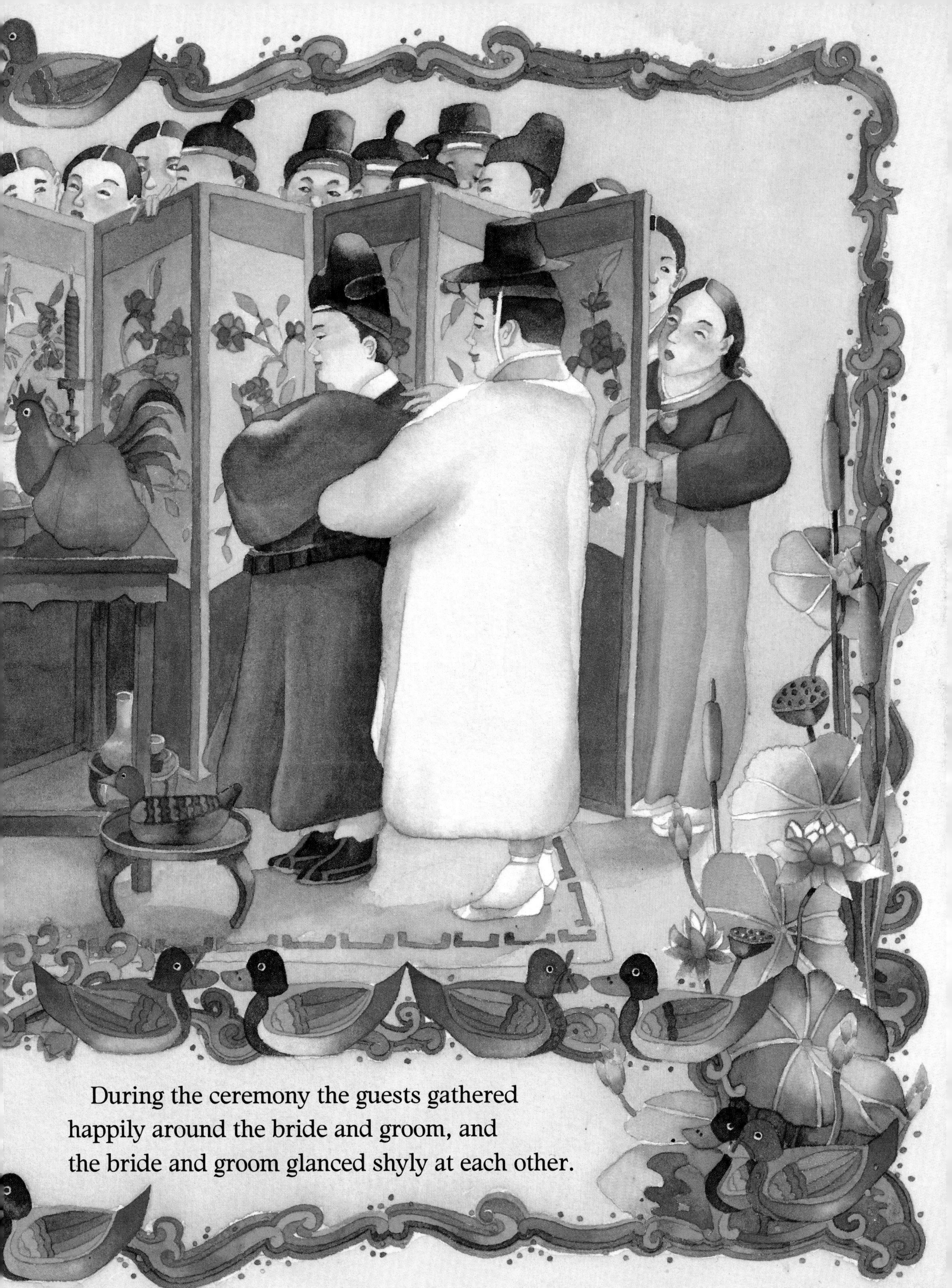

During the ceremony the guests gathered happily around the bride and groom, and the bride and groom glanced shyly at each other.

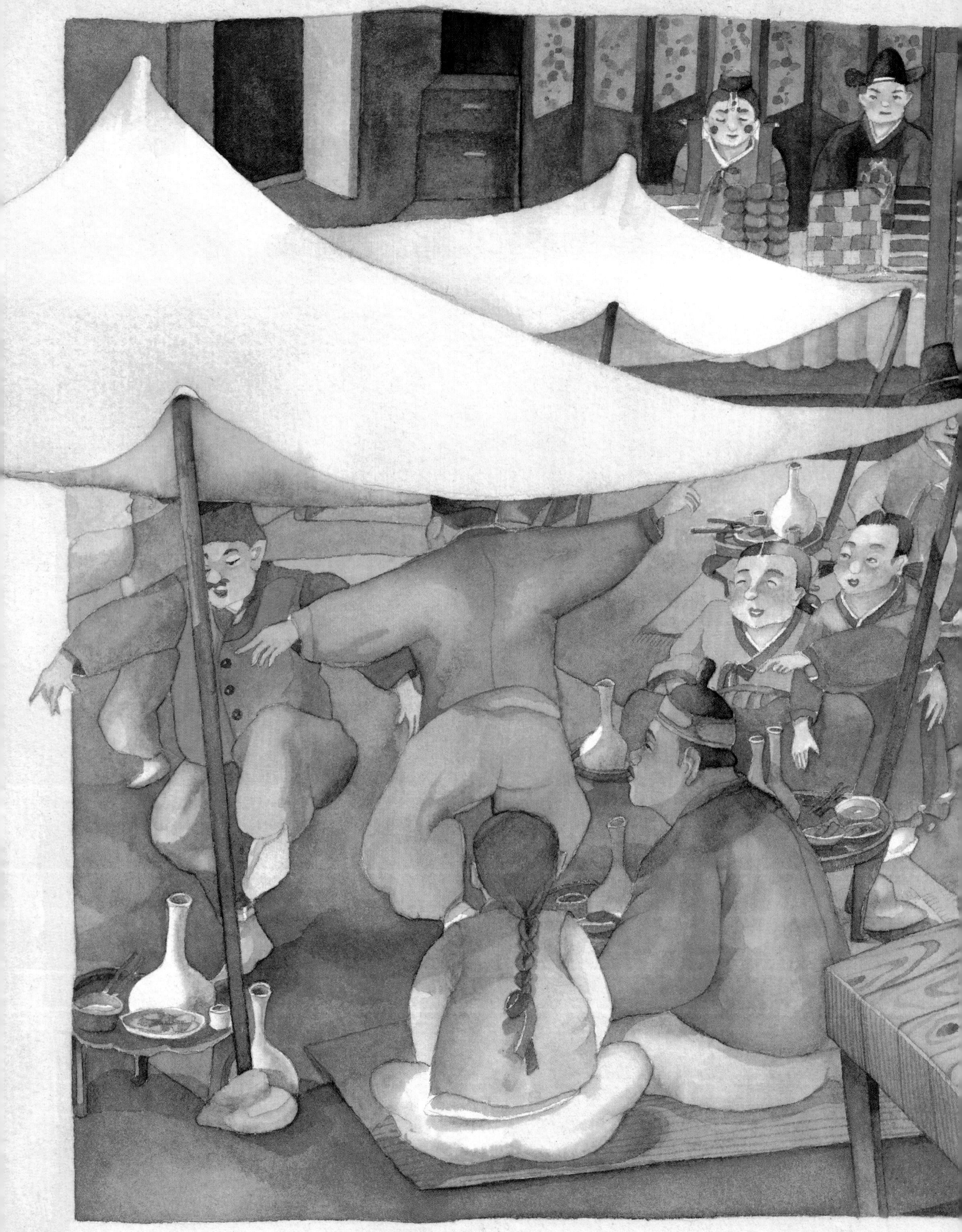

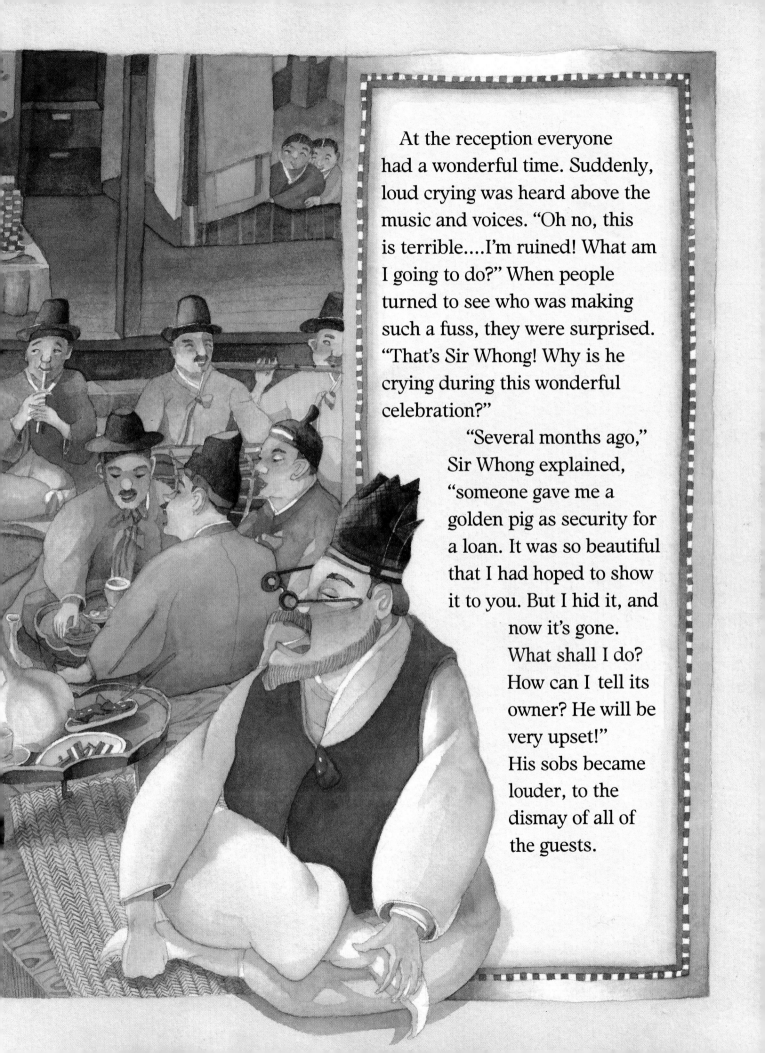

At the reception everyone had a wonderful time. Suddenly, loud crying was heard above the music and voices. "Oh no, this is terrible....I'm ruined! What am I going to do?" When people turned to see who was making such a fuss, they were surprised. "That's Sir Whong! Why is he crying during this wonderful celebration?"

"Several months ago," Sir Whong explained, "someone gave me a golden pig as security for a loan. It was so beautiful that I had hoped to show it to you. But I hid it, and now it's gone. What shall I do? How can I tell its owner? He will be very upset!" His sobs became louder, to the dismay of all of the guests.

Sir Whong's story spread quickly, as he knew it would, and soon reached the town where the stranger lived.

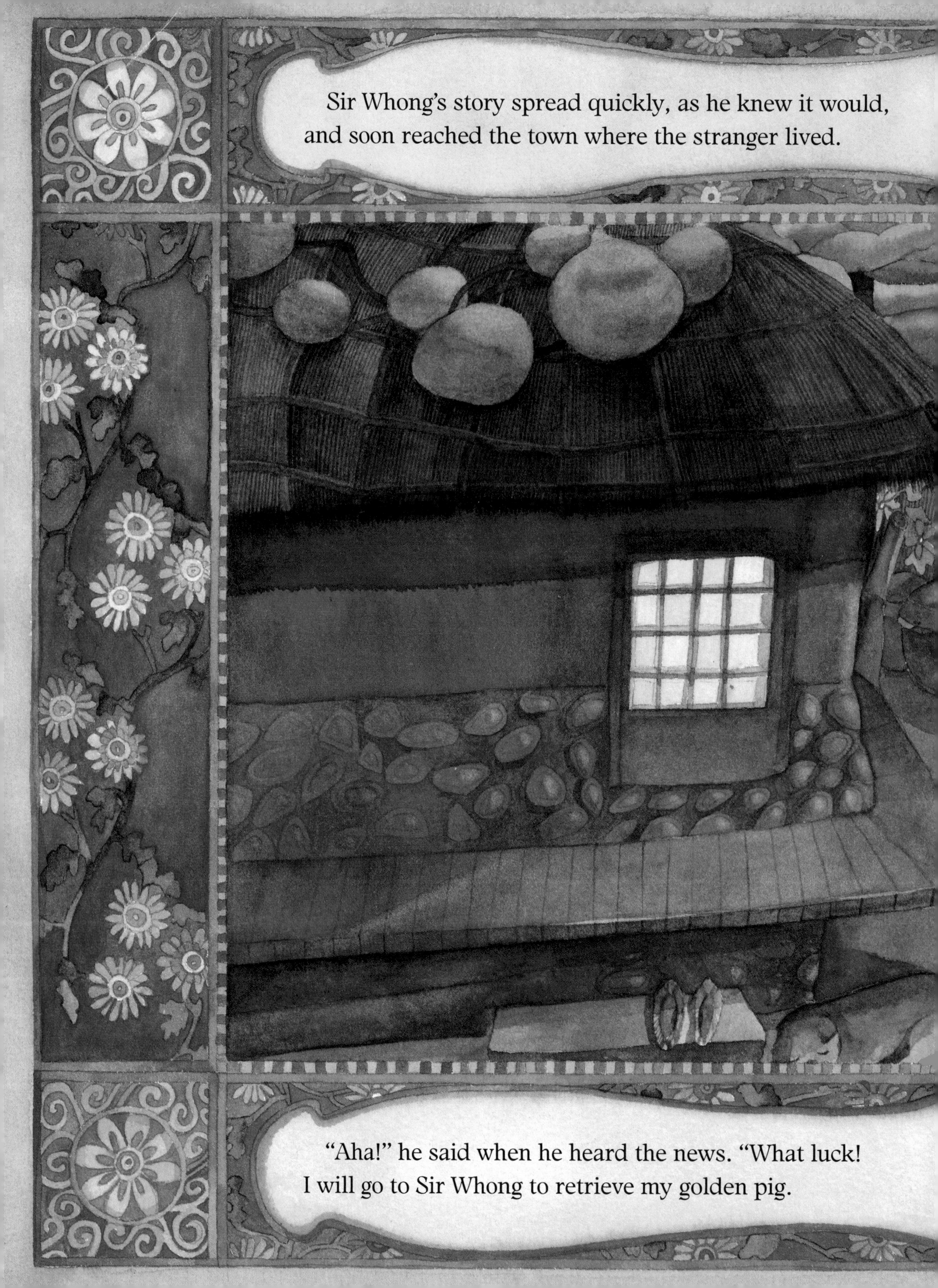

"Aha!" he said when he heard the news. "What luck! I will go to Sir Whong to retrieve my golden pig.

"Since he no longer has it, I am sure that he will be willing to pay for it. Now, how much should I charge?"

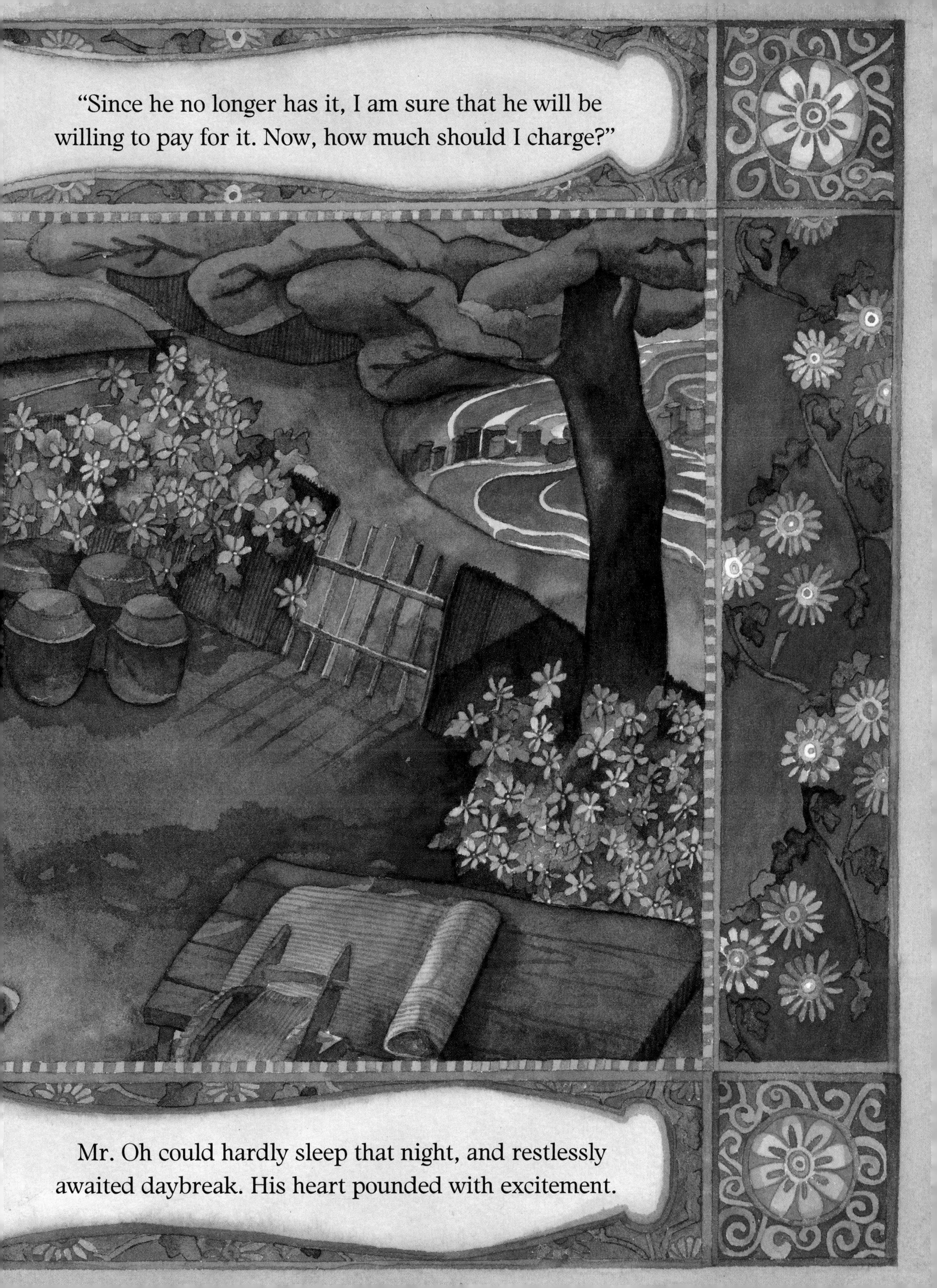

Mr. Oh could hardly sleep that night, and restlessly awaited daybreak. His heart pounded with excitement.

Almost before the sun came up the next day, the stranger made his way to Sir Whong's house. He said, "Sir Whong, I have been able to come up with the money that I owe you sooner than expected. Thank you for your kindness. My poor, old mother is much better now." Mr. Oh praised Sir Whong for his charity.

Sir Whong graciously accepted his compliments, and placed the money in his safe.

Then the stranger said, "Well, I have a long trip ahead of me. May I please have my treasure back?" "Of course," said Sir Whong. "Here it is. I've kept it safe in my closet for all of these months." Sir Whong took out the box and opened it. Mr. Oh was astounded. Sir Whong had had the "golden" pig all along! Suddenly Mr. Oh realized that it was *he* who had been tricked.

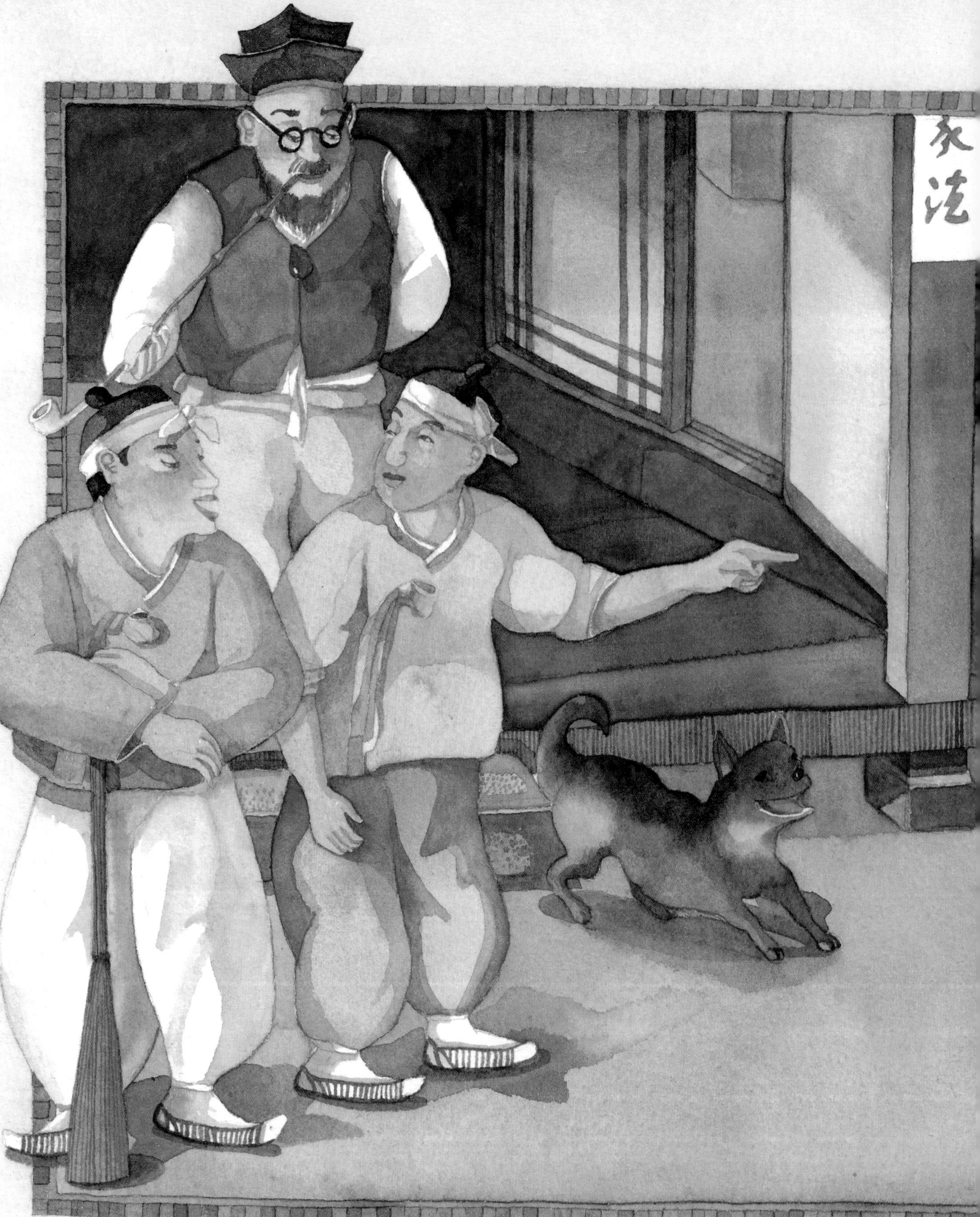

His face reddened, and he cried out in embarrassment. Then he turned and ran away as swiftly as he could. The villagers did not see or hear from him again.

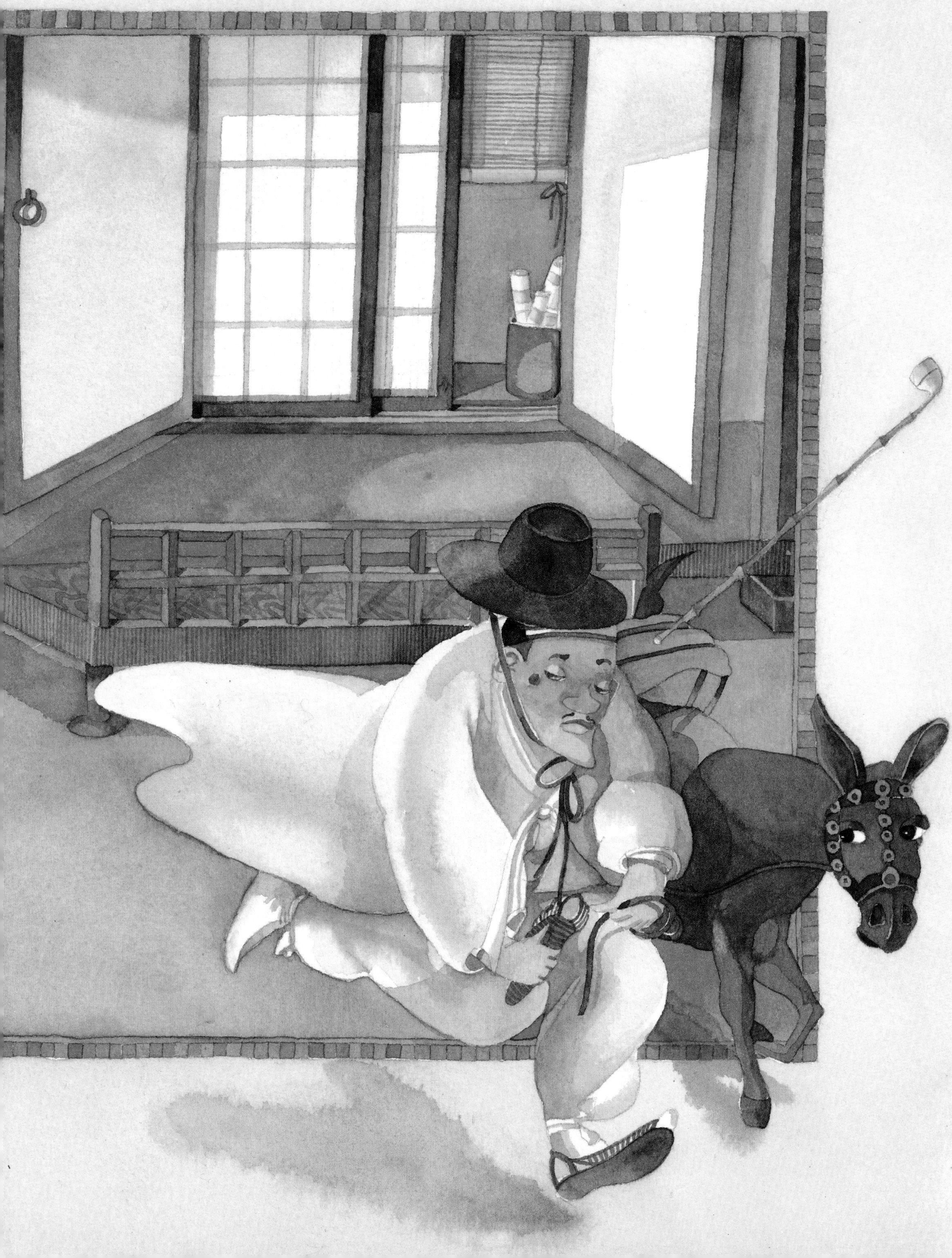

Mr. Oh never imagined that his downfall would be caused by Sir Whong's humor and wisdom. The village was peaceful once more, and Sir Whong lived happily, his fine reputation secure forever.